Also by Nancy Wood

Poetry

MANY WINTERS

WAR CRY ON A PRAYER FEATHER

HOLLERING SUN

Photography

TAOS PUEBLO

THE GRASS ROOTS PEOPLE

HEARTLAND NEW MEXICO: PHOTOGRAPHS FROM THE
FARM SECURITY ADMINISTRATION, 1935–43

IN THIS PROUD LAND (WITH ROY STRYKER)

Fiction

THE MAN WHO GAVE THUNDER TO THE EARTH

THE KING OF LIBERTY BEND

THE LAST FIVE DOLLAR BABY

Nonfiction

WHEN BUFFALO FREE THE MOUNTAINS

COLORADO: BIG MOUNTAIN COUNTRY

CLEARCUT: THE DEFORESTATION OF AMERICA

A Doubleday Book for Young Readers

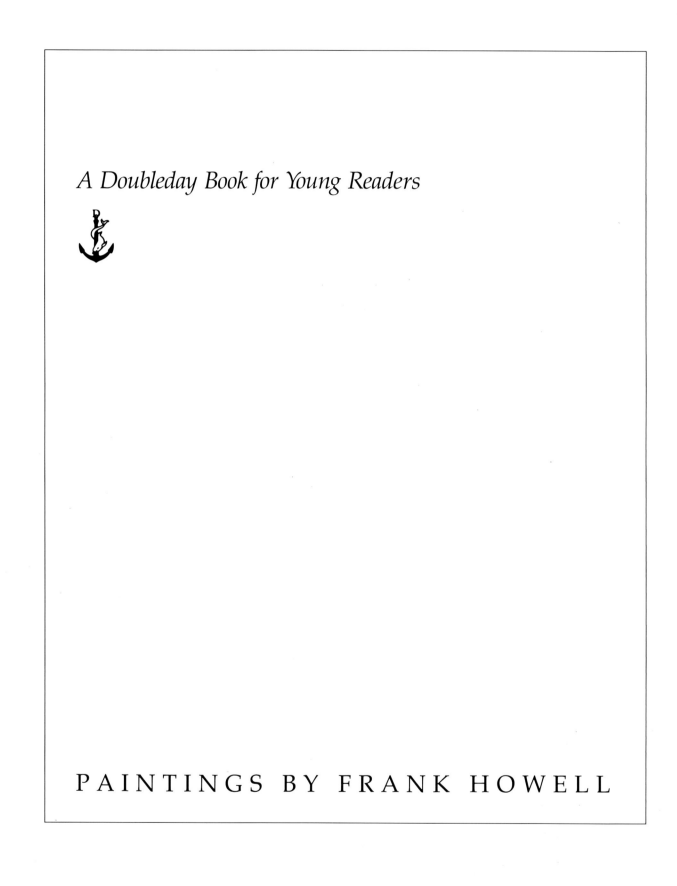

PAINTINGS BY FRANK HOWELL

Spirit Walker

POEMS BY NANCY WOOD

A Doubleday Book for Young Readers
Published by
Delacorte Press
Bantam Doubleday Dell Publishing Group, Inc.
1540 Broadway
New York, New York 10036

Library of Congress Cataloging in Publication Data
Wood, Nancy C.
Spirit walker : poems / by Nancy Wood ; paintings by
Frank Howell.
p.   cm.
Summary: The author's poems reflect the deep spiritu-
ality and values of the Taos Indians and their inter-
connectedness to the earth.
ISBN 0-385-30927-9
1. Taos Indians — Juvenile poetry.   2. Children's poetry,
American.   [1. Taos Indians — Poetry.   2. Indians of
North America — Poetry.   3. American poetry.]
I. Howell, Frank, ill.   II. Title.
PS3573.O595S66   1993
811'.54 — dc20   92-29376   CIP   AC

This book is set in 12-point Palatino Medium.
Design by Lynn Braswell
Manufactured in the United States of America
October 1993
10   9   8   7   6

To Carolyn Johnston,
Katherine Parker,
Juanita Marcus Turley, and
Neale Ward,
women warriors all.

Strawberry's Summer

Preface

Ever since the publication of *Many Winters* in 1974, readers from all over the world have written to express their feelings about the book. Some have told me how the poems helped them through the death of a loved one. Others have read the poems at memorial services, weddings, and bar mitzvahs. A group of Carmelite monks wrote to say they had incorporated poems from *Many Winters* into their liturgical mass. The poems have appeared in countless anthologies and textbooks, even a Unitarian hymnal. *Many Winters* has touched a universal chord, as strong now as it was when it was first published a generation ago.

Now, twenty years after completing *Many Winters*, artist Frank Howell and I have decided to produce a companion piece, *Spirit Walker*, which explores some of the themes raised in the previous volume. These poems, like the others, are based on my long association with the Taos Pueblo Indians, who shared their deep spirituality. From the time I first met them, in 1961, I was impressed by their values and by an unshatterable outlook that stemmed from their interconnectedness to the earth as a living whole. Was it possible for me, a white woman, to understand these values? For years I merely observed, absorbing what I could. Slowly my perceptions and, ultimately, my way of life began to change.

What did it take to become "in tune" with Indian beliefs far removed from my Judeo-Christian background? Learning to listen, for one thing; letting go of old, worn-out cultural ideas, for another. Solitude was necessary if I was ever to learn anything, so I retreated to the mountains for long periods of time. I still live that way, twenty miles from Santa Fe, at the edge of an old Spanish land grant. Loneliness is part of the lesson, my teacher Red Willow Dancing used to say. Empty your heart and mind. Do not become distracted.

But that was the catch. I *was* distracted — by the realities of having to support four children. After a time the children left, my life moved into a middle-age phase, my consciousness expanded. Distraction meant taking time to watch a red-tailed hawk soaring above my house or witnessing the drama of huge clouds rolling down from any one of the four mountain ranges I can see from my window. This is what matters now, acquiring what the Indians call the quiet heart. In so doing, I have learned to live life from the inside out.

We all are a part of something largely undefinable, call it God or the Great Spirit, Buddha or Allah, Krishna or Mozart. I feel connected to this mystery on rivers, in deserts, and on the sea, but mostly in the mountains. Twice a year, at summer solstice and again at autumnal equinox, I make a pilgrimage to the top of Independence Pass, at twelve thousand feet in the Colorado Rockies.

As I am perched on top of the world, my ritual never changes. I carry a portable tape deck, tapes of beloved Vivaldi, the Mozart horn concerti, and Beethoven's Triple Concerto, and hike out across the tundra until I am far away from people. I choose a spot on the knife-edge ridge that forms the division between the eastern and western watersheds of the country. There I unpack a long, billowing purple silk dress from my day pack and slip it over my parka and jeans. The music of Vivaldi plays to the wind, and I dance, on and on along the Continental Divide in my hiking boots, paying homage to the mountains, renewing my claim to a stubborn, persistent force that anchors me to this earth. Here is where I am free. Here is where I bend to examine, with a geologist's loupe, a tiny yellow flower no bigger than the head of a pin, and weep because the Great Spirit has seen fit to create such perfection.

This is what Red Willow Dancing meant about interconnectedness. A blade of grass was where he said God lived; the wind was the breath of the Great Spirit, renewing us once again. To me, this is what life is all about.

There, between earth and sky, suspended in time, I begin to understand.

Nancy Wood
Santa Fe, New Mexico
April 1992

Introduction

The pueblo of Taos is the most spectacular of all nineteen Indian villages along the Rio Grande. High in the lush mountains of northern New Mexico, Taos is an architectural jewel, four and five stories high, made of straw and mud, with a river running down the middle. The village looks primeval, an anomaly amid the surge of cars and tour buses that come nearly every day of the year.

East of the pueblo rise the mystical Sangre de Cristo Mountains. The cosmology of the Indians began high in these mountains where they emerged from Blue Lake and found the Four-Legged Animals and the Winged Creatures willing to help them. The Indians believe their sacred knowledge comes from this lake; every August the entire tribe makes the arduous trek to give thanks to the spirits who guide them, and to ask their help in personal and tribal matters.

To the west the immense Rio Grande Valley stretches as far as the eye can see. The mighty Rio Grande surges through the valley, cutting a deep gorge that looks like a miniature Grand Canyon. Out of this desert landscape, which once belonged to them, the Taos created legends; here, too, they drove off Navajos, Apaches, and Utes who tried to invade their flawless domain centuries ago.

A rich, deep, and complex religion, drawn from mountains, desert, sky, animals, and birds, sustains the Indians. Nothing is possible, they say, without the Great Spirit who infuses everything with life and meaning. To this end every waking moment is spent cognizant of natural circles, where ants play as great a role as eagles, and the lessons of bears and caterpillars are one and the same.

Today the Taos are still governed by ancient laws and customs, a complex belief system that has seen them through seven centuries in their mud village. The Taos insist that their village sprang from the earth like a mushroom and that it contains sacred spirits of ancestors and animals alike. Though hardly anyone lives in the ancient village anymore, it is a shrine, and they allow no electricity or plumbing; outsiders are not permitted once the sun goes down and the Indians depart in their pickup trucks, having spent the day selling their wares in the plaza. However, each family maintains an apartment in the old village and uses it for feast days, weddings, and funerals. The village remains the core of their existence. Each summer, the Indians painstakingly restore it.

Native Americans have lived in this area for thousands of years, but the arrival of the Spanish in the late sixteenth century dramatically changed their lives. Friars brought the Catholic religion with its incomprehensible concepts of sin, guilt, and redemption. Spanish food such as chili and tortillas, Spanish language, customs, and dress, and, of course, the miraculous horse were introduced by wave after wave of conquistadores. While many pueblos succumbed to disease, fled to the desert, or merged with other tribes, the Taos remained successfully where they were, defeating all attempts to remove them. They became surface Catholics, but inwardly, and in their kivas, their Indian religion prevailed.

Nearly four hundred years of occupation, first by Spain, then by Mexico, then by the United States, nonetheless forced an irreversible cultural upheaval. Now, near the end of the twentieth century, the Taos still live in the same magnificent surroundings, but even that is changing. Modern government houses are sprouting up outside the ancient village walls; cars and trucks have all but eliminated the need for the horse; electricity has crept up to the edge of the old village. Moreover, the ancient Tiwa language is rarely spoken by the young people, who eschew wearing blankets, braids, or moccasins, unlike their older counterparts. Yet a strong thread unites them. In times of crisis the Indians band together. They are still fighting for survival: now economic pressure is forcing many to leave the village and seek opportunity elsewhere.

Inside the crumbling adobe walls, where the religious life takes place, not much has changed. Old men wrapped in blankets sit in the sun, watching the distant peaks. They speak their singsong Tiwa language and tell stories they first learned as children. Old women wrapped in shawls haul water from the river. There is a stillness here, despite the clamor, a rhythm as old as the mountains towering above. This mystery is what draws visitors from all over the world.

In their life-affirming isolation, tapping into beliefs that take them far beyond petty strife, the Indians are able to return to a time when they came out of Blue Lake and found the world was good. For many, that is all that truly matters now, when conflict, as well as cultural pride, are forcing them to examine their own deep roots.

Oglala Woman

Ten Million Stars

Inside each raindrop swims the sun.
Inside each flower breathes the moon.
   Inside me dwell ten million stars,
   One for each of my ancestors:
   The elk, the raven, the mouse, the man,
   The flower, the coyote, the lion, the fish.
Ten million different stars am I,
   But only one spirit, connecting all.

Face of the Waters

Emergence

Before we came out of the lake,
   we did not know illness.
Before we came out of the lake,
   we did not know death.
Before we came out of the lake,
   we did not know evil.
We needed our emergence
   to accept them.

The Story of a Flower

In the season of wild strawberries
    I came from the earth as a flower
    High on a hill above my village, with only
The Eagle, the Buffalo, the Bear, and the Butterfly
To watch the petals of my spirit unfold.

The Eagle spoke first. He said:
    Sister, you will never have wings like me,
    Except in the pathways of your dreams,
Yet you will fly to the top of the sky
Because I give you the Gift of Courage.

The Buffalo spoke next. He said:
    Sister, you will never survive a long time like me,
    Except on the trail of your memories,
Yet you will see a thousand winters go by
Because I give you the Gift of Endurance.

The Bear spoke next. He said:
   Sister, you will never know the secrets
   Of the Four-Legged Animals, since you are only a flower,
Yet the knowledge of all creatures is yours
Because I give you the Gift of Wisdom.

The Butterfly spoke next. She said:
   Sister, you believe you are very important,
   Because the creatures have given their gifts to you,
Yet here on this hill you will always be at home
Because I give you the Gift of Humility.

So I have lived for many seasons,
   Among the Eagle, the Buffalo, the Bear, and the Butterfly,
   Watching the birds go by, speaking to rain and sky.
My colors have been the colors of the rainbow.
My beauty has given joy to all who see me.

To bloom even when there is no rain
   Requires the Courage of the Eagle.
To last through the heavy snows of winter
   Requires the Endurance of the Buffalo.
To understand the importance of all seasons
   Requires the Wisdom of the Bear.
But to rejoice when my blossoms die
   Requires only the Butterfly's Humility.

Mother's Words

Why look for answers, my child,
Among the people you meet?
Why believe there is fulfillment
In your narrow life of work?

Why sacrifice the gift of loneliness
To fill up the time with diversion?

Look inside every living thing you find.
Feel the energy of rocks and leaves, hummingbirds
and cactus.
Dwell for a moment in a single blade of grass.
Discover the secret of snowflakes.

In these patterns lie harmony, my child.
In harmony, the universe.

Our Children

Our children are like flowers to us.
Each one different.
Each one beautiful.
Each one growing strong with us.

Our children are like stars to us.
Each one sparkles.
Each one moves through the universe.
Each one closer to the heart of us.

Our children are like life to us.
Each one precious.
Each one unpredictable.
Each one having to let go of us.

Sedona Autumn

The Earth Called to My Friend

The Earth called to my friend and he went,
    Deep into the Earth Root from which he came,
    Down into Blue Lake where our ancestors dwell,
Deep into the heart of the Yellow Corn Maiden,
To a place of beauty and light.

I watched the sky for a long time and then I saw
    A cloud in the shape of my friend,
    Riding a fine white horse with wings so big
They blotted out the sun, making shadows
Across my withered fields of corn.

I called to my friend to ask if he was happy
    And if he knew more than when he left.
    I called out his name and blessed him
With an eagle feather, dancing in his behalf,
The wild old dances of our youth.

    Good-bye, my friend, I said, watching the clouds
    Crumble into little pillows that fell as rain
    Into the dryness of my fields.

Red Feathers in a Salmon Sky

Love

For us, my love,
    The faraway moon laughed
    And breathed a new song
    For all the earth to hear.

For us, my love,
    The stars deserted the sky
    And became a silver pathway
    To our dreams.

For us, my love,
    Time made a ladder out of grass
    To show us to our happiness.

For us, my love,
    Beauty encircled two lives and
    Love created one horizon.

Women, You Must Learn to Be Warriors

Women, you must learn to be warriors
   Now when times are dark and our men
   Are afraid to tell us what is in their hearts.
   There is so much trouble in our land
   That it is up to you to decide
   Which direction the wind must blow.

Women, you are our tree of life
   Just as you were a long time ago
   When a man said: carry my seed.
   If you go forth from this darkness,
   Telling our story of courage and survival,
   Then our tree will grow strong with your words.

Women, do not worry about tomorrow.
   Even when daylight is long in coming,
   The sun remembers its place in the sky.
   Take this blue shawl of knowledge and
   Wrap it around your daughters, telling them
   That women must not be afraid to be warriors.

Of Mountains and Women

The hearts of mountains
   and the hearts of women
Are both the same. They beat to
   an old rhythm, an old song.

Mountains and women
   are made from the sinew of the rock.
Mountains and women
   are home to the spirits of the earth.
Mountains and women
   are created with beauty all around.
Mountains and women
   embrace the mystery of life.

Mountains give patience to women.
   Women give fullness to mountains.
Celebrate each mountain, each woman.
Sing songs to mountains and to women.
   Dance for them in your dreams.

The spirit of mountains and of women
Will give courage to our children
   Long after we are gone.

Earthen Fruit

Earth Roots

What are Earth Roots, my daughter asked
   when she was just a child,
examining each flower in its home.

Earth Roots are a special connection,
   a sacred thread that joins our spirits
   to every living thing, I said. Earth Roots
Join me to you, and you to birds and flowers.

In her hand my daughter held a sparrow
   with a broken wing. She said:
Can Earth Roots make the sparrow fly again?

The sparrow can become a rose, in time,
   just as the rose takes wing, I said.
Earth Roots make all things possible.

My daughter did not understand these things
   until she had a daughter of her own.
   Then she saw the way Earth Roots join
   The sparrow to the rose.

Spirit Shield

Pueblo Reflections

When a feather falls at your feet, it means you are to travel on wings of curiosity. Don't be afraid of strange lands or a language you don't understand. The feather means freedom. Why else do you think the bird gave it to you?

What cannot be changed must be accepted.
What is accepted must be endured.
Back when we were a people on foot, running up and down the mountains, we lost our advantage. People took our land, our children. We accepted everything, except the loss of our children. When you look at us now you will see a big hole in our hearts. This is so our children can climb back in.

We go out to your world and come back, trying to decide which way to go. The young travel to places they think will give them everything. After a while, they come home. They stand in the plaza, looking up at the mountains, seeing our ancestors. We older ones say nothing. Isn't silence better than a scolding?

We Shall Live Again

For a long time, people have been telling us,
    We're finished. Used up. Devoured by a world
    anxious to make us into copies of themselves.
Our education was supposed to wipe memory
    from our minds. A new language was supposed
    to make us forget old songs, old stories.
Automobiles and television were meant to carry us
    to new horizons where we would find
    the answer to our fears.
People laughed at our old ways. They tried
    to learn our secrets. They traded whiskey
    for wisdom. They promised us our land and rivers
    forever. If only we would listen.
Finally they said: why are you not dead?
We said: on the outside we may be just like you.
    But deep inside where our spirit dwells,
    We carry the thread of our ancestors.
        We shall live again.
        We shall live.
        We shall.

The Lesson of the Striped Wolf

On a night so dark I thought the stars had died, a Striped Wolf came to my bed and this is what he said:

Brother, you have forgotten the ways of the ancestors we had in common long ago when wolves and men were one.

With his gleaming yellow eyes Striped Wolf looked into my face and gave me light to see how cluttered my path had become.

Brother Wolf, said I, if we are of the same blood, the same bone, the same spirit, why do I believe that life would be easier if only I had money?

Easy, said Striped Wolf as he took my hand and led me out the door. Wolves hear deeper rhythms than men can hear and so they dance even when there is no music. Wolves walk a Pathway of Knowledge around the Earth. They know the language of Stars. Striped Wolf offered his breath to the night, and a part of him rose to the sky.

When I awoke, moonlight filled my house with diamonds as big as fists. Striped Wolf only laughed when I gathered my treasure in a bag, believing I was rich.

Fool, said he, only men believe that pieces of the moon are worth anything. A Striped Wolf knows illusion when he sees it. When he emptied my bag, nothing but dust fell out. Now you must live with your foolishness, he said as he ran outside to greet the dawn. In his paws he caught golden rays of sunlight and used them as a ladder to climb to the part of the sky he had not visited yet.

As for me, I no longer look for riches in pieces of moonlight. Instead I cultivate my fields and there I become strong with the power of Striped Wolf's knowledge.

Deer Dancer

Elk Dreamer

Elk Dreamer, in your robe of a hunter's ancient quarry,
Elk Dreamer, standing tall against the ruined mountains,
Elk Dreamer, alive with memories of old hunts,
    What do you remember?

I remember the hunter's quest for humility,
I remember the animal's gift of generosity,
I remember telling you, a long time ago,
There are no destinations in the hunt,
    Only hidden paths among the ruins.

The Web of Life

To kill the owl
   is to kill
   the mountains in their majesty.
To kill the bear
   is to kill
   the beauty of all living things.
The web of life
   connects grass to fish
   trees to turtles
   sky to caterpillars.
The web of life
   connects me to everything
   that came before,
   even to the moment
   when earth herself was born.
To break the web of life
   is to fill the universe
   with pain.

Knowing the Earth

To know the Earth on a first-name basis
   You must know the meaning of river stones first.
Find a place that calls to you and there
   Lie face down in the grass until you feel
Each plant alive with the mystery of beginnings.
   Move in a circle until you discover an insect
   Crawling with knowledge in its heart.
Examine a newborn leaf and find a map of a universe
   So vast that only Eagles understand.
Observe the journey of an ant and imitate its path
   Of persistence in a world of bigger things.
Borrow a cloud and drift high above the Earth,
   Looking down at the smallness of your life.
The journey begins on a path made of your old mistakes.
   The journey continues when you call the Earth by name.

The Planting of Mother Earth's Navel

Every spring, when the ice breaks on the creek
   And our long sleep ends, a powerful man
   Goes forth to the sacred center of our village.
He stands there, enjoying the awakening land,
   Greeting the return of Father Sun,
   Asking him to bless our fields
   And for the rains to come and our crops to be good.

This is the time for the Planting of Mother Earth's Navel,
   A time for seeds to be carried into her sacred core,
   A time for the source of all our blessings
To be honored by songs and celebration. The Planter
   Of Mother Earth's Navel is a holy man, an elder who
   Stands with his seeds and waits
   For Mother Earth's Navel to hear his greeting. Then

Down, down into the center of Mother Earth's Navel he goes,
   To the place where dark becomes light, to tender green,
   And in this place finds reverence. One by one, he plants
Seeds of hope and regeneration into the deep sweet body
   Of Mother Earth. When the Holy Planter is finished, we rejoice,
   Knowing that our crops shall grow tall because
   We have planted Mother Earth's Navel with our dreams.

The Earth Is All That Lasts

The Earth is all that lasts.
On and on in loneliness
The dry Earth cracks and opens
Bleeding dust and bones
Healing itself through time
Moving across its tortured skin.

Oh patient Earth so restless
You are in weakness strong.
Within the mountain of your ashes
Lies the river of my fire.

Oh weeping Earth reborn
With the death of living men
Let your strength flow into me
And my cry become your song.

The Earth is all that lasts.
The Earth is everywhere in me
Even when I'm gone.

Messages

Summer and Winter People

We are a Summer People and a Winter People,
    Planters and hunters, gatherers of
    Small rewards for the pain of all our efforts.

We are a Summer People and a Winter People,
    Living and dying, Sun Bringers and
    Sun Takers for each cycle of our seasons.

We are a Summer People and a Winter People,
    Dressed in leaves and stones, dancers for
    The blessings of Earth and all her creatures.

We are a Summer People and a Winter People,
    Working and resting, keepers of dreams and
    Our Mother Earth connections.

We are a Summer People and a Winter People,
    Dwelling amidst hummingbirds and snowflakes, makers of
    Experience to hand down to our children.

Fruit from the Light

Spirit Walker

Spirit Walker, with long legs poking out of rain clouds
   Along the mesa tops,
   Listen to our prayers for understanding.
Spirit Walker, with strong arms embracing the wounded Earth,
   We ask forgiveness for our greed.
Spirit Walker, with footsteps echoing like promises
   Across the aching land,
   Give Fire and Ice to purify us.
Spirit Walker, with tears that fall as Snow and Rain,
   Heal our forests and our rivers,
   Our homes and the hearts of all creatures.
Spirit Walker, heed the cry of every living thing
   And bathe the Earth with harmony.

Warrior's Prayer

Generations

In the days when there were no days
And the nights were not counted yet
There were these Generations:

The Grandfather, who created us,
Drew his breath from the Sun's energy
Then placed his lips upon the seed
Of Birds, of Animals, of Men.

The Grandmother issued stars and moon
From her breast of sacred light,
Offered the mystery of sky
And the healing robe of night.

The Father, who is the Living Sun,
Scattered darkness before him,
Then announced the growth of root and bone
With the coming of each dawn.

The Mother became the Enduring Earth.
Naming Wind and Fire and Water,
She gave life to Generations
And harmony to stones.

The Children passed from hands of parents,
Gathered up root and bone,
Embraced the world with laughter

Then showed the Grandfather in.

Unity

We have grown together you and I
Like two trees I saw once
Sharing a common root.
One tree gave shade,
The other light.
The trees grew strong and tall together.
They protected one another.
One tree was home to the other.
One tree was always looking out.
They endured the cold together.
They lived when there was no rain.
The trees shared sunlight and sky.
They shared earth and water.
The trees that I saw once
Grew together until at last
When winter came they died
And went back to the earth as one.

A Change of Worlds

When a man dies, he is not dead.
    He has merely changed his World instead.
His vision may become that of a Tall Tree,
    Looking out in all directions at once.
His vision may become that of a Tiny Ant
    With his nose as his horizon.
His vision may include the voice of Stars or
    The humming song of Leaves. Who knows?

In this World a man can also be
    The warm breath of the Summer Wind
    Or the comforting blanket of Winter Snow.
In this World a man who is a Raven
    Is also a man who is a Stone.

Each living thing has lived before:
The Bird. The Tree. The Man.

Why fear this change of Worlds, my friend?
    Your courage travels with you.
    Your example is left behind
    So that others may know
        The sweetness of your time.

Grandmother's Gift of Fire

The Wisdom of My Grandmothers

The wisdom of my grandmothers
    traveled on the wings of stars
To the place where my village slept
    beneath a rain of darkness.
The wisdom of my grandmothers
    blew on the wind from the east,
    creating dreams of harmony.
The wisdom of my grandmothers
    flowed down from the mountaintop
    through memories of circles unbroken
    by wider circles of doubt.
The wisdom of my grandmothers
    brushed the life-giving feathers
    of those who danced with feet of stone,
    lifting them like eagles
    to the waiting arms of the wind.

Three Sisters

We are the Three Sisters of Fire and Earth and Water.
  Without us, nothing lives or grows.

We are the Three Daughters of Sun and Moon and Stars.
  Without us, no path exists through the universe.

We are the Three Wives of Birds and Trees and Animals.
  Without us, there would be no wings or roots or bones.

We are the Three Mothers of Clouds and Wind and Rain.
  Without us, our children would go hungry.

We are the Three Friends of Beauty.
  Without us, flowers would look like stones.

We are the Three Grandmothers of Wisdom.
  Without us, men would only speak of war.

We are the Three Aunts of Endurance.
  Without us, what would survive?

Passing Storm

Solitude

Do not be afraid to embrace the arms
   of loneliness.
Do not be concerned with the thorns
   of solitude.
Why worry that you will miss something?

Learn to be at home with yourself
   without a hand to hold.
Learn to endure isolation
   with only the stars for friends.

Happiness
   comes from understanding unity.
Love
   arrives on the footprints of your fear.
Beauty
   arises from the ashes of despair.
Solitude
   brings the clarity of still waters.
Wisdom
   completes the circle of your dreams.

The Circle

All is a circle within me.
    I am ten thousand winters old.
    I am as young as a newborn flower.
    I am a buffalo in its grave.
    I am a tree in bloom.
All is a circle within me.
    I have seen the world through an eagle's eyes.
    I have seen it from a gopher's hole.
    I have seen the world on fire
    And the sky without a moon.
All is a circle within me.
    I have gone into the earth and out again.
    I have gone to the edge of the sky.
Now all is at peace within me.
Now all has a place to come home.

Two Worlds

For us, there are Two Worlds of Being.
The First World is the outer world we live in,
A shell that encases the body, an attitude
That stifles the mind and pretends
That money is the measure of worth.

The First World is harsh, though comfortable,
Alluring, though vain. It is the popular world
Where everyone longs to be, yet once they arrive,
They dream of a new direction. In this world,
Everything costs something and what is free costs more.

The First World is one of wheels and destinations,
Membership dues and limitations. It is a sanctuary
For those who desire conformity in all things.
Here duplicate people wearing duplicate clothes
Speak a language without meaning, and think thoughts
Without substance to their form.

The First World is where everyone lives, yet
No one actually survives. It is an acceptable address
Where you forfeit all that you are for what
You will never become and what you are not
Is what you want those around you to remember.

The First World has power, but no strength.
It is one of mirrors, but no reflection.
In this world, there is success, but no mystery.
Goals, but no journey. In this world,
Boundaries keep ideas from colliding.

The Second World is the inner world of harmony,
Where you can go anytime your spirit aches for company.
Here you can listen to the songs of rocks and leaves and
Embrace the wisdom of rivers and essential things contained in
Raindrops or a flower's belly or the earth's warm breath of spring.
In this world, beauty is companion to mystery.

The Second World is one of joy and curiosity,
A connecting thread to birds and oceans, plants and animals.
The Second World is one of children's laughter, women's songs,
Men's stories, the essence that remains long after the experience
Has passed on. In this world, all circles return.

The Second World is where you can travel
On the wings of dreams or the tails of newborn stars.
This world is revealed though a rainbow's colored eyes,
Or in a spider's silver road between two leaves,
Or even in silence, the kind that follows ecstasy.
The Second World is able to survive without the First,
But the First World cannot last long without the Second.
The Second World offers meaning to existence
While the First World offers existence only.
Between these two Worlds
Lies reason, the seam that connects one World to another.
The Second World is yours for no money.
The First World is yours for no effort.
Which one will you choose?

We Come as Clouds

We come as clouds, the Buffalo and the Badger
   Of our memory, lingering
   on the endless rooftop of the earth.

We come as clouds, the Hummingbird and the Eagle
   Of our forgotten youth, remembered
   In the wide daylight of our dreams.

We come as clouds, our ancestors preserved
   In one enormous pathway, remaining
   Forever in the wind currents of our minds.

We come as clouds, a flowing picture of our history
   Circling the earth like a promise,
   So that we see ourselves forever in the sky.

Silences–Tsankawi

Out there in the caves of remembrance
   on the mesa where sandstone footsteps
   wear a path of wonder in the mind,
I heard my first silence.
                    It was merely
a pinpoint of stillness, isolated
   from the desert wind and the sound
                      of my own breathing.

             In silence
I heard the whisper of ancient people
   making robes and grinding corn
   as if it were
A matter of life to them.
              In their muffled words
I recognized the shadows of my own language,
   not even spoken by my children anymore.
I heard these ancient people telling tales
   of visitors from the south,
   carrying parrots, and of the time
                 they first saw
                 the sun grow dark at noon.
In this silence I learned much
   about the silences that nature gives
   to remind us
               of our nothingness.

The Old Man Born of Dreams

You must not be afraid to travel
   where there are no roads.
You must not give in to the darkness
   when there is no sign of light.
You must not be afraid to grow wings
   when you are tired of the ground.
You must not be afraid to swim
   when you are nothing but a stone.
If experience is the child born of risk, then
   acceptance is the old man born of dreams.

Pecos Autumn

All as It Was in This Place Timeless

All as it was in this place timeless.
All as it was between the human soul and the earth.
For there is no difference between
The life of a man and the life
     Of all growing things.
Who is to say if a man
Shall not be a tree instead?
We pray to all of nature and do it no harm.
These are our brothers
     All men and all animals and all trees.
Some part of ourselves
Is in earth and sky and everywhere.
     It shall continue
As long as nature follows its own purpose.
     It shall continue
As long as we know what we are doing here.

Never Shall I Leave

Never shall I leave the places that I love.
Never shall they go from my heart
Even though my eyes
     Are somewhere else.

Santa Fe Sky

Waiting

From the impoverished strength of youth
  We begin our journey to the other side of life,
  Gathering experience as we go along,
  Knowing nothing except that the way is long
And filled with the unexpected.

From the exhausted strength of old age
  We look back and wonder at the journey,
  So long, so hard, yet we have our memory
  Of beauty in each step we took,
Not the void that follows after.

Whispers

The world comes closer to my village every day,
    In automobiles and airplanes,
    With noise and desperation,
Seeking solutions in dust and shadows.
What shall I tell these people?
    To forget the world out there?
    To live as we do, afraid, yet brave?
    Shall I teach them how
    To die a little death each day?
Or shall I create a world they'll never know,
Filled with storytellers and eagles,
Great hunters and painted warriors?
No. I can only tell them whispers.
    Endure.
    Endure.
    Endure.

My Help Is in the Mountain

My help is in the mountain
   where I take myself to heal
   the earthly wounds
   that people give to me.

I find a rock with sun on it,
   and a stream where the water runs gentle,
   and the trees which one by one
   give me company.

So must I stay for a long time,
   until I have grown from the rock,
   and the stream is running through me,
   and I cannot tell myself from one tall tree.

Then I know that nothing touches me,
   nor makes me run away.
My help is in the mountain
   that I take away with me.

Sky Garden

Native Blessing

Bless these, our circumstances.
   Bless the hardship and the pain.
Bless the hunger and the thirst.
   Bless the locusts and the drought.
Bless the things which do not turn out right.
   Bless those who take all and give not.
In these circumstances, find growth.
In growth, discover clarity.
In clarity, an inner vision.

One People

In the beginning my people were one people.
They were made of feathers and bone.
My people rode the tail of the sun
And swung on a rope through the sky.
My people lived inside the earth
On water running backwards into time.

Indian Apocalypse

The day the grass stopped growing
   Was the day the buffalo died.

The day that rivers ran with fire
   Was the day that forests fell.

The day that spring turned brown
   Was the day that Mother Earth
   Gave birth to birds without wings.

The day that mountains crumbled
   Was the day the eagle rose
   And painted the sun with blood.

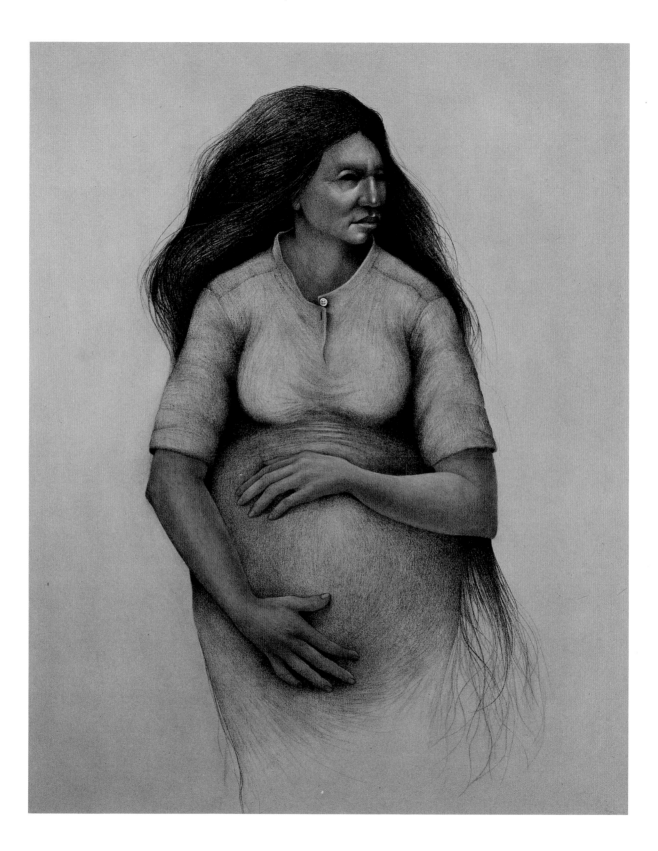

New Mexico Rose

A Woman's Lesson

A woman's lesson is a simple lesson:
   Whatever life asks, answer with love.

A woman's lesson is a wise lesson:
   Whenever conflict threatens, go forth in harmony.

A woman's lesson is an enduring lesson:
   Whatever is taken from you, give back in generosity.

A woman's lesson is a gradual lesson:
   Whenever there is a storm, remain a calm center.

A woman's lesson is a courageous lesson:
   Whenever there is despair, sow the seed of hope.

A woman's lesson is a practical lesson:
   Wherever there is dryness, go and get the rain.

What Women Are. A Legend.

Women are made of feathers.
   Just look.
That's why there are so many
   Beautiful birds around.
Women came into the world determined.
   Just look.
They noticed the trees were bare
   And so they grafted
   Green leaves to empty branches.
Women danced wherever they went.
   Just look.
They made friends with wind
   To make the flowers bend
   And to stir new songs from stones.
Women are meant to sing all the time.
   Just listen.
   That's why water plays an endless tune
   And trees whisper secrets to the moon.

Spirit Brothers

Have you ever seen Old Man Rock,
    the one with Crows in his hair,
keeping watch over forests and streams?
Have you ever seen the Woman of the Mountains,
    her face turned toward the sky,
lying forever among old memories?
Have you ever seen a Buffalo Cloud or one
    that looks like a Pig chasing after a Sheep?

These are our Spirit Brothers, the ones who
    never die, telling us the way to live now
when all the world is upside down with fear.
In our dark night of loneliness, Old Man Rock
    gives courage to our shattered dreams.
In the blinding light of uncertainty, the Buffalo Cloud
    offers encouragement.
In the black dawn of emptiness
    the Woman of the Mountains
    drains our cup of fear.

Next time you see Old Man Rock, remember:
    He once lived the same life you live now.
    When he died, his Spirit Brother
    gave direction to the Winds.

Next time you see a Buffalo in the Sky, remember:
    He once lived as all creatures live now.
    When he died, his Spirit Brother
    gave brilliance to the stars.

We are all Spirit Brothers. The Woman. The Man.
    The Buffalo. The Tree. The River.
    Each is part of another.
    Each is part of the same.

Crow Messenger

Dream Ravens

Ravens of my dreams,
    Cure the anger in my heart.
Ravens of my indecision,
    Make straight the path before me.
Ravens of my memory,
    Let your song come unto me.

As my brothers fly above the earth
    So must I leave my importance behind.
As my sisters sing songs of rejoicing
    So must I find a courageous voice.

Ravens, let there be peace among us.
    May we fly as one idea.
Ravens, give memory to my dreams
    So that I may hear the voices
    Of my ancestors telling me
    That all the world is changing
And my fears will turn to leaves.

River Matrix

The Way to Understanding

Within and around these mountains,
    your good fortune will be returned to you.
Within and around these mountains,
    your peace will be returned to you.
Within and around these mountains,
    your freedom will be returned to you.
Within and around these mountains,
    your beauty will be returned to you.
All things return to those
    who pray for understanding.
All things depart from those
    with anger in their hearts.

Index of Titles

All as it was in this place timeless   61
Change of worlds, a   45
Circle, the   53
Dream ravens   77
Earth called to my friend, the   21
Earth is all that lasts, the   37
Earth roots   27
Elk dreamer   33
Emergence   15
Generations   43
Indian apocalypse   69
Knowing the earth   35
Lesson of the striped wolf, the   31
Love   23
Mother's words   18
My help is in the mountain   65
Native blessing   67
Never shall I leave   61
Of mountains and women   25
Old man born of dreams, the   59
One people   68
Our children   19
Planting of mother earth's navel, the   36
Pueblo reflections   29
Silences–Tsankawi   58
Solitude   51
Spirit brothers   74
Spirit walker   41
Story of a flower, the   16
Summer and winter people   39
Ten million stars   13
Three sisters   49
Two worlds   54
Unity   44
Waiting   63
Way to understanding, the   79
Web of life, the   34
We come as clouds   57
We shall live again   30
What women are. A legend.   73
Whispers   64
Wisdom of my grandmothers, the   47
Woman's lesson, a   71
Women, you must learn to be warriors   24